Which Pet Is Best?

Parent's Introduction

Welcome to **We Read Phonics**! This series is designed to help you assist your child in reading. Each book includes a story, as well as some simple word games to play with your child. The games focus on the phonics skills and sight words your child will use in reading the story.

Here are some recommendations for using this book with your child:

1 Word Play

There are word games both before and after the story. Make these games fun and playful. If your child becomes bored or frustrated, play a different game or take a break.

Phonics is a method of sounding out words by blending together letter sounds. However, not all words can be "sounded out." **Sight words** are frequently used words that usually cannot be sounded out.

② Read the Story

After some word play, read the story aloud to your child—or read the book together, by reading aloud at the same time or by taking turns. As you and your child read, move your finger under the words.

Next, have your child read the entire story to you while you follow along with your finger under the words. If there is some difficulty with a word, either help your child to sound it out or wait about five seconds and then say the word.

③ Discuss and Read Again

After reading the story, talk about it with your child. Ask questions like, "What happened in the story?" and "What was the best part?" It will be helpful for your child to read this story to you several times. Another great way for your child to practice is by reading the book to a younger sibling, a pet, or even a stuffed animal!

> This time, let's take turns reading.

> OK, but you start.

LEVEL 2 **Level 2** introduces simple words with short "e," short "o," and short "u" (as in *get*, *hot*, and *bug*). All consonants except "q" are used at this level. Special sounds include "ck" (as in *lock*), "wh" (as in *when*), "ar" (as in *car*), and "s" as the "z" sound (as in *bugs*).

Which Pet is Best?

A We Read Phonics™ Book
Level 2

Text Copyright © 2010 by Treasure Bay, Inc.
Illustrations Copyright © 2010 by Erin Marie Mauterer

Reading Consultants: Bruce Johnson, M.Ed., and Dorothy Taguchi, Ph.D.

We Read Phonics™ is a trademark of Treasure Bay, Inc.

Published by
Treasure Bay, Inc.
P.O. Box 119
Novato, CA 94948 USA
Printed in Singapore

Library of Congress Catalog Card Number: 2009930771

Hardcover ISBN: 978-1-60115-321-0
Paperback ISBN: 978-1-60115-322-7

We Read Phonics™
Patent Pending

Visit us online at:
www.TreasureBayBooks.com

PR 11-09

Which Pet Is Best?

By Bruce Johnson

Illustrated by Erin Marie Mauterer

Picture Walk

Help prepare your child to read the story by previewing pictures and words.

What is she holding in this picture?

That's a mop!

1. Turn to page 4. Point to and say the word *pets*. Ask your child to point to the pets in the picture.

2. On page 5, read the words ". . . but which pet is best?" Ask your child to point to the pets in the picture.

3. Turn to page 6. Point to the picture. Ask your child what pet is in the picture. Ask more questions until your child answers *dog*. Ask your child to point to the word *dogs* on the page.

4. Continue "walking" through the story, asking questions about the pictures or the words. Encourage your child to talk about the pictures and words you point out.

5. As you move through the story, you can also help your child read some of the new or more difficult words.

Sight Word Game

Go Fish

Play this game to practice sight words used in the story.

1 Write each word listed on the right on two plain 3 x 5 inch cards, so you have two sets of cards. Using one set of cards, ask your child to repeat each word after you. Shuffle both decks of cards together, and deal three cards to each player. Put the remaining cards in a pile, face down.

2 Player 1 asks player 2 for a particular word. If player 2 has the word card, then he passes it to player 1. If player 2 does not have the word card, then he says, "Go fish," and player 1 takes a card from the pile. Player 2 takes a turn.

3 Whenever a player has two cards with the same word, he puts those cards down on the table. The player with the most matches wins the game.

4 Keep the cards and combine them with other sight word cards you make. Use them all to play this game or play sight word games featured in other **We Read Phonics** books.

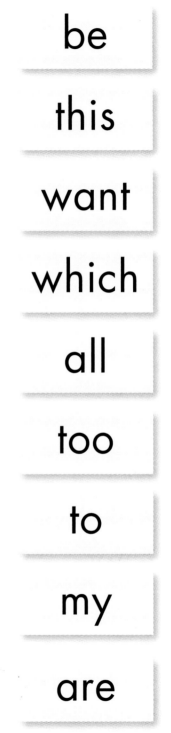

be

this

want

which

all

too

to

my

are

Pets can be fun,

. . . but which pet is best?

Big dogs run fast,

. . . but this pup can hop.

Cats can bat balls,

. . . but cats want snacks.

What if I get this pet?

I must get the mop!

I can let this pet run.

This pet is a hat!

I want this duck,

. . . but ducks want a pond.

Is this a pet rock?

This pet hid in the rocks.

I want this pet too.

It wants to be my pet.

I must get this pet!

It hops on my hand.

Which will be the best pet?

Can I get ten pets?

Yes, I will get all ten!

Pets are the best!

Phonics Game

I Spy

Help your child to recognize beginning sounds.

I spy something that begins with the same sound as dig.

Is it a dog?

1. Explain to your child that these words begin with the "s" sound (make the sound for "s"): *sound, sack, sag, snack, sip, sit, sap,* and *sand.*

2. Ask your child to say a word that begins with the same beginning sound as *sand.*

3. If your child has trouble, offer some possible answers or repeat step 1 with other simple words.

4. When your child is successful, say: "I spy something that begins with the same sound as *pet.* What is it?" Possible answers: *pup, pop, popcorn, pocket, pin, pot, picture,* or *peas.* (Ideally, you are spying something that your child can also see.)

5. Repeat step 4 with the following words: *big, dogs, fast, cats, get, mop, hat,* and *rock.*

Phonics Game

I Am Thinking

Blending letter sounds together helps children learn to read new words.

I am thinking of something . . .

1. Think of a one-syllable person, place, or thing from the book.

2. Say: "I am thinking of something from the book that has these sounds, (Make the first letter sound, then the second letter sound, then the third letter sound.) What is it?"

3. For example, for the word *pet,* say: "I am thinking of something from the book that begins with 'p' (instead of saying the letter, make the sound for 'p'), then the sound 'e' (make the sound for short 'e,' as in *set*), and then the sound 't' (make the sound for 't'). Can you guess what it is?"

4. If your child has difficulty, you can offer some possible answers. Say: "I am thinking of something from the book that has these sounds, 'p'. . . 'e'. . .'t.' It could be *pup, pet,* or *cat.* Do you think it is *pup, pet,* or *cat*?

5. Continue with additional words from the story. For variation, ask your child to take a turn, and ask you to guess a word.

If you liked *Which Pet Is Best?*
here is another **We Read Phonics**™ book you are sure to enjoy!

Where Is My Frog?

A pet frog is on the loose, creating havoc wherever he hops! This easy-to-read story offers non-stop fun and excitement, as a boy chases the frog from one crazy mishap to the next.